Marty Frye, Private Eye

Marty Frye, Private Eye

Janet Tashjian

Illustrations by Laurie Keller

A
LITTLE
APPLE
PAPERBACK

SCHOLASTIC INC.

New York Toronto London Auckland Sydney
Mexico City New Delhi Hong Kong

For Josh Levison—a true poet
—J. T.

To my grandmother, Evelyn Luella
—L. K.

No part of this publication may be reproduced in whole or in part, or stored in a retrieval system, or transmitted in any form or by any means, electronic, mechanical, photocopying, recording, or otherwise, without written permission of the publisher. For information regarding permission, write to Henry Holt and Company, Inc., Attention: Permissions Department, 115 West 18th Street, New York, NY 10011.

ISBN 0-439-09557-3

Text copyright © 1998 by Janet Tashjian.
Illustrations copyright © 1998 by Laurie Keller.
All rights reserved.
Published by Scholastic Inc., 555 Broadway, New York, NY 10012,
by arrangement with Henry Holt and Company, Inc.
SCHOLASTIC and associated logos are trademarks and/or registered
trademarks of Scholastic Inc.

12 11 10 9 8 7 6 5 4 3   0 1 2 3 4/0

Printed in the U.S.A.   40

First Scholastic printing, November 1999

CONTENTS

Marty Frye, Private Eye

The Crime

It was recess,

and Marty Frye was hungry.

He climbed his favorite tree.

He began to peel an orange.

His classmate Emma stopped him.

"Come down!" she yelled.

"Someone stole my diary,

and you have to find it!"

Marty put his orange away.

He climbed down the tree.

He gave Emma his card.

It was written in crayon on the back
of a milk carton.

"This is so messy, I can hardly read it,"
Emma said.

"Does it say PET detective?"

"No," Marty said.

"Does it say PLANT detective?"

"No," Marty repeated.

"Does it say PILOT detective?"

"NO!" Marty screamed.

"It says POET detective.

I make up rhymes

while I solve your crimes!" he added.

"I don't care how,

but I want my diary now!" Emma yelled.

"Hey, maybe I'm a poet too."

Marty opened his top-secret

detective backpack.

He took out his green pad and pen.

"Give me the facts.

So I can follow the tracks," he said.

"Well," Emma explained. "My diary is blue.
It has a brass lock and key."
Emma showed him the key.
It was on a chain around her neck.
"I miss my diary already.
It's full of all my thoughts and secrets."

Marty wanted to eat his orange.

He wanted to sit in the tree

and read his poetry book.

But business came first.

"I'll be glad to look

for your missing book," he told Emma.

Searching for Clues

First Marty searched Emma's desk.

He found her markers,

her brownie,

her friendship bracelet,

her juice box,

her golf ball,

her jacks,

her chewed-up pencil,

her eyedropper,

even her collection of Barbie shoes.

But not her diary.

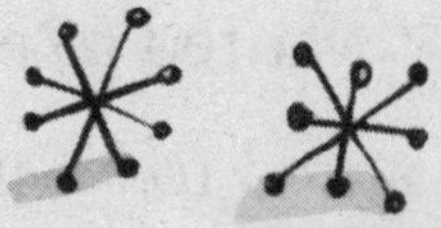

Marty asked Emma when she had seen it last.

"I had it with me at lunch," she said.
"I remember because I almost spilled
milk on it.
I also had it with me when Mr. Ditz
told us about the movie.
But it wasn't there
when the movie was over."

Marty liked the movie they had seen in class.

It was about the sun and moon.

When the movie first started,
the projector was too low.

The solar system shone on the floor.

When Mr. Ditz went to fix the projector,
he walked on the moon.

After he fixed the projector,
the moon filled the screen.

Watching a movie was good.

Listening to Mr. Ditz was not.

Now Marty wondered.

Did someone steal Emma's diary
while the classroom was dark?
Did someone want to know Emma's secrets?

It was time to ask
some questions.

The Suspects

Pete sat in front of Emma in class.

He liked to take things.

He took Marty's poetry book last week.

"When we watched the movie," Marty asked,

"did you happen to see

a small book with lock and key?"

Pete shook his head.

"I was too busy

tossing paper clips at the screen."

Marty looked around Pete's desk.

He found a pile of paper clips.

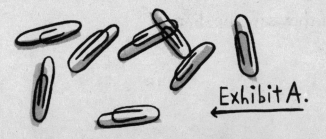

← Exhibit A.

Marie sat next to Emma.

"Excuse me," Marty said politely.

"I'm busy," Marie answered.

Marty took her crayons away.

"I'll keep it brief.

Are you the thief?" he asked.

Marie grabbed her crayons back.

"NO!" she said.

Then Marty asked Linda,

and Tommy,

and Luke,

and Val,

and Kimmy,

and Joey the Sneeze

if they saw the diary.

"NO!" they all screamed.

Marty made a list of all the people
who might have stolen Emma's diary.
Billy Gately was first on the list.
He always teased Emma.
Last week he hid a dead butterfly
in her tuna fish sandwich.
Emma found it just in time.
She thought it was yellow lettuce.
Billy just might be the thief, Marty thought.

"Hello, Mr. Gately.

Read any good books lately?"

Marty asked.

"No," Billy said.

"They ran out of horror books at the library."

Marty leaned in closer.

"I was thinking more of a personal story,

not the kind that's really gory,"

Marty rhymed.

Billy shook his head.

"I don't like that kind of stuff."

"Well you've got some explaining to do
because I see a book that's blue."
Marty pulled a blue book from Billy's desk.
It was full of scribbled green ink.

Goblins and vampires filled the page.
Billy grabbed the book back.
"Hey, that's my journal for Ms. Barrett's class.
What's your problem, anyway?" Billy said.

Emma whispered to Marty,
"My diary is smaller than that.
It's a darker shade of blue.
Plus, my handwriting is much neater
and I don't draw monsters."
"You could have told me before.
Those kind of details are hard to ignore,"
Marty replied.
He hated making false arrests.

The Search Continues

Marty asked Emma if anyone
had been looking at her diary.
"Well, Lee kept asking me about it,"
Emma said.
"She wanted one for her birthday,
but she didn't get one."
Lee was still outside for recess.
Marty followed her from the swing set,
to the hopscotch,
to the basketball court,
to the fence,
to the lunch area.

She pulled a blue book from her bag.

She crouched over on the table

and began to write in the book.

"Aha!" Marty said.

"Caught in the act, and that's a fact!

Hand over the diary."

"NO!" Lee hollered.

She held on to the book with all her might.

So did Marty.

"You're in a real dilemma,

because this book belongs to Emma."

"Emma?" Lee asked. "This is my diary.

I made it from a pad

and covered it with blue paper."

She looked at the ground.

"I wanted a real diary for my birthday,

but I got a bike instead."

Marty didn't feel bad for her.

His own bike had a flat tire.

He hadn't used it in weeks.

He was a good detective

but a bad repairman.

Marty apologized to Lee.

He sang her "Happy Birthday"

to make up for his mistake.

Emma approached Marty.

"Where's my diary?" she asked.

"The whole class could have read it by now."

Marty smiled.

"I've hit some dead ends,

but I hope we're still friends," he replied.

"We're not!" Emma said.

"I want my money back."

"You gave me no fee.

I'm doing this for free," Marty said.

27

"Well, you're a lousy detective,"
Emma scolded.

Marty thought and thought.

Where was the best place to look for a book?

The library, of course.

They hurried down the hall.

Marty asked the librarian for help.

"Have you seen something small and blue?

It's a diary, Mrs. Drew."

"No," Mrs. Drew answered.

"But have you checked the lost and found?"

Marty emptied out the box on the shelf.

He found a left boot,

a red mitten,

a broken comb,

a nickel (which he claimed),

a bag of acorns,

a compass,

and a belt.

The closest thing to a diary

was a comic book.

He kept that for evidence.

Mrs. Drew told Marty the new poetry books

would be in on Friday.

Marty hoped he would solve his case by then.

"Any luck?" Emma asked.

Marty shook his head.

"We don't have much time.

Back to the scene of the crime,"

Marty shouted.

Aha!

Marty examined the room again.
He took a roll of yellow ribbon
from his detective kit.
He roped off the area around Emma's desk.
Now he could study the crime scene.
Maybe he could even dust for fingerprints.
Mr. Ditz came back into the classroom.
Marty had wanted to solve the case
at recess.
Now he would have to put in for overtime.
Marty watched everyone take a seat.
He watched Kimmy sit in the back row.
She couldn't see the board,
so she took a book from the shelf
and sat on it like a booster seat.

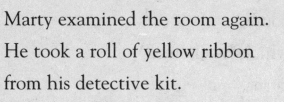

Maybe the thief wanted Emma's diary

for another reason besides reading.

Marty suddenly remembered the movie

and Mr. Ditz walking on the moon.

He hurried to the projector.

It was on an empty desk

in the middle of the room.

It was propped up on a small blue book.

Marty lifted the projector.

Underneath it was Emma's diary.

"Here's your book.

There is no crook!" Marty shouted happily.

Emma leaped with joy.

"My top-secret diary. Thank you!"

Mr. Ditz stepped over the yellow ribbon.

He looked at the diary.

"Emma, is that yours?

I needed a wedge for the projector.

Your book was the perfect size.

I'm sorry. I should have asked," Mr. Ditz said.

Marty handed the book back to Emma.

But it fell on the floor.

SMACK!

When Marty picked the diary up,

the lock was open.

He flipped through the pages of the diary.

"To be perfectly frank,

these pages are blank," Marty said.

"This is embarrassing," Emma confessed.

"But I don't really write in my diary.

I just like using the little key."

She put the key in the lock and turned it.

When it clicked shut, she smiled.

A Job Well Done

Another case solved.

Marty took the orange

from his pocket.

Maybe now he could finish his snack

and read his poetry book.

"Hey!" Emma pointed to the orange.

"I bet you can't think of a rhyme for that!"

Marty peeled the fruit and took a slice.

"Orange is alone in the no-rhyme zone."

He took another bite.

Solving cases always made him hungry.

The Crime

Marty walked home from school.
He was glad he could help
his friend Emma today.
He walked by the hardware store,
the clothing store,
and the fire station.
He climbed up the tree in front
of the ice-cream shop.
It was his favorite view of town.

From his perch, he could see

Mr. Lipsky's toy store.

Mr. Lipsky stood on the sidewalk.

He was shaking his head, looking sad.

Marty climbed down the tree and walked over.

He asked Mr. Lipsky what was wrong.

"I'm missing a box of toys," Mr. Lipsky said.

"They were brand-new Action Chuck dolls."

Marty couldn't believe it! Action Chuck!

Marty loved Action Chuck.

Action Chuck was a truck driver on TV.

He drove around the country

and stopped bad guys.

Marty watched his show every week.

He gave Mr. Lipsky a smile and said,

"Mr. Lipsky, with some luck,

you'll soon be holding Action Chuck."

Marty followed Mr. Lipsky inside.

Searching for Clues

The store was full of giant panda dolls,

woodpecker puzzles,

baseball bats,

skateboards,

polka-dot beach balls,

magic tricks,

and poster paints.

But most of all, the store was full of people.

Some waited in line, some waited for help.

Some waited to play with toys.

LiZard BOY

Magic TRICKS →

Can I get him? Can I? Can I?

"If you give me the scoop,

I can start to snoop," Marty told Mr. Lipsky.

"The truck came after lunch,"

Mr. Lipsky explained.

"They delivered six boxes.

Two boxes were filled with puppets,

another with books.

The fourth box was full of games and balloons,

and the last two were Action Chuck boxes."

Mr. Lipsky walked over to a stack of boxes.

"Now there's only one box of Action Chucks."

Mr. Lipsky opened a box with his knife and

took out an Action Chuck doll.

Marty's favorite—the one with the

driving gloves and removable sunglasses.

"Twenty-four of these dolls are missing,"
Mr. Lipsky said.
"I can't get another shipment
for two months.
So many children will be disappointed."
Marty asked Mr. Lipsky who else
was working in the store.
"My son, Peter, and a new boy, Tom,"
he answered.
Marty got up from his chair.
"Let's get to work.
Where's the new clerk?" he asked.

The Suspects

Mr. Lipsky and Marty found Tom.

He was stacking shelves with games.

Mr. Lipsky introduced Tom to Marty.

Marty waved, and Tom climbed

down the ladder.

"Where were you today around two?"

Marty asked.

"I was here," Tom answered.

"Helping Mr. Lipsky with the new shipment."

"When you unloaded the truck,

did you see Action Chuck?" Marty asked.

Tom got very excited.

"Action Chuck is the greatest!" he said.

"My friends and I watch his show
all the time."

Marty and Tom talked about how cool
Action Chuck was.

They talked about the two-way radio
in his thermos.

They talked about the secret laser
in his rearview mirror.

Then Marty remembered
he was supposed to be solving a case.

"I must find the crate
before it's too late," he declared.

Marty looked around.

He liked this store.

He liked Mr. Lipsky's other store too.

It was near Marty's grandmother's house.

Sometimes she took Marty there for a treat.

Marty always pretended he didn't
want anything.

His grandmother always bought him
something anyway.

Mr. Lipsky finished with his customer.

"Let's go find my son."

He took Marty into the back room.

"Peter!" he called.

No one answered.

"That's strange," Mr. Lipsky said.

"He should be here."

"I'll sit and wait.

He won't be late," Marty said.

"Good idea," Mr. Lipsky replied.

"Describe your son,

so I'll know he's the one," Marty rhymed.

Mr. Lipsky told Marty his son had brown

glasses, blond hair, and a beard.

Then Mr. Lipsky went back into the store.

Marty waited for Peter Lipsky.

The Search Continues

While he waited, Marty looked around.

He looked on the shelves.

He looked in the closet.

There were lots of action figures
but no Action Chucks.

He checked the bulletin board.

There were notes reminding Mr. Lipsky
to order new games.

Notes reminding him to bring toys
to the other store.

Notes reminding him to call his son.

Mr. Lipsky needs a lot of reminding,
Marty thought.

Marty sat on a box and took out his poetry book,

the new one with poems about railroads.

A few minutes later, Tom came into the room.

Marty hid behind a box.

He took his spyglass from his backpack.

He had made it with old tubes and foil.

He watched Tom dial the phone.

"The action figures are ready," Tom said.

"You can pick them up tonight."

Tom hung up the phone.

Marty popped up from behind the box.

"You should have confessed.

Now you're under arrest!" he shouted.

"What are you talking about?" Tom asked.
"That was the children's hospital.
We have boxes of old toys to give them."
Marty felt bad that he had blamed Tom.
But he was glad the hospital
would get some toys.
Marty returned to snooping.
Soon he heard a noise outside.
He pulled a box over to the window
to stand on.
Marty searched the parking lot.
He saw a young man with blond hair
and a beard.
He wore glasses.
This must be Peter Lipsky.
He was putting a large box into
the trunk of his car.
Marty tiptoed outside to get a better look.

Aha!

Marty hid behind the stairs.

He watched Mr. Lipsky's son

tie the box down.

The stamp on the side of the box said

Marty ran across the parking lot.

He looked Peter in the eye.

"You can't steal from your dad.

That would be very bad," he scolded.

Marty yelled to Mr. Lipsky in the store.

Mr. Lipsky hurried outside.

Peter tried to explain.

Marty interrupted and told him to be quiet.

He opened the trunk of the car.

He showed the box to Mr. Lipsky.

Mr. Lipsky was very mad.

"Where are you taking these?"

he asked his son.

Peter sat Mr. Lipsky down on the stairs.

"You left me a note," Peter said.

"You told me to take this box

to the other store."

Mr. Lipsky scratched his head.

"I don't remember that," he said.

Peter took a note out of his pocket.

He showed it to his father.

He showed it to Marty.

It said,

Bring one box of Action Chucks to other store.

Mr. Lipsky studied the note.

"I guess I did write that," he said.

"I am so busy, I forgot."

Peter gave his father a smile.

"It's okay," he said.

Peter looked at Marty.

Peter was not smiling.

"I would not steal from my father," Peter said.

Marty wished he had not wrongly
accused Peter.

But he was glad he found the missing toys.

"Give me a break.

I made a mistake," Marty said.

He held out his hand.

Peter shook it.

This time, Peter and Marty both smiled.

A Job Well Done

Marty helped Peter pack up the box in the car.

"Wait a minute," Mr. Lipsky said.

He took out his knife.

He opened the box.

He took out an Action Chuck doll

and handed it to Marty.

"Thanks for helping me find these," he said.

Marty beamed.

On his way out, Marty had an idea.

"Perhaps I can do something more.

I'd like to help you in your store."

Mr. Lipsky told Marty

he could stop by anytime.

"We need all the help we can get," he said.

Marty told Mr. Lipsky he would

see him tomorrow.

Then he walked toward home.

He was glad Action Chuck was with him.

Not that he needed any help stopping crime.

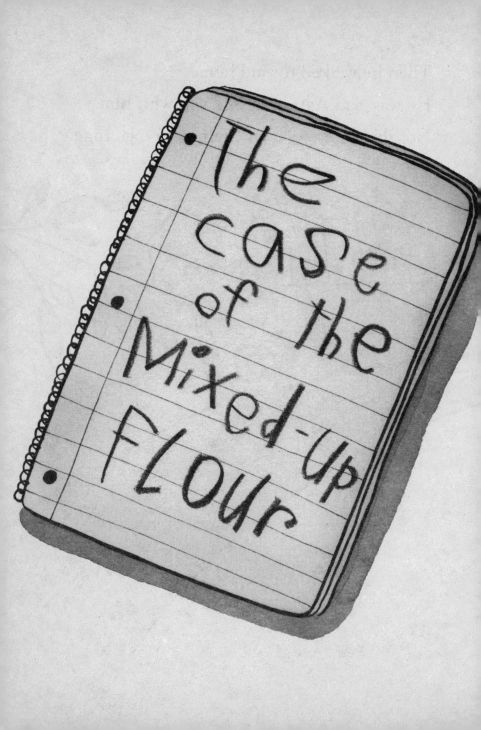

The Crime

Marty read his poetry book and
ate his after-school snack.
(Chocolate cookies and milk.)
Action Chuck sat on the table.
Marty's mother mixed butter
and sugar in a bowl.
She turned on the oven.
She asked Marty about his day.

He told her about finding Emma's diary.
He told her about helping Mr. Lipsky
at the toy store.
"Sounds like a busy day," his mother said.
Marty's sister, Katie, ran into the room.
Her hair was red.
Every other day, her hair was blond.
Marty figured she had been painting.
He was a detective, after all.
"Someone took my flour!" Katie shouted.
"It was a present from Jackie!"

"I haven't seen it," Mrs. Frye said.

"Maybe it's in your room."

"No," Katie said.

"It was on the table.

Now it's gone!"

Marty looked at the clock.

"I might have time

for one more crime," he said.

He took his plate to the sink.

He washed his hands.

He followed Katie downstairs

to the playroom.

Searching for Clues

Marty took out his pad.

He told Katie to tell him everything.

Katie took a deep breath.

"Jackie and I painted after school,"

she explained.

Katie showed Marty their paintings.

One looked like a clown with dandruff.

Another looked like a car with mice.

"Then we decided to make some goop,"

Katie continued.

"Jackie brought over a bag of flour."

Marty had seen Katie make goop before.

She squished it between her fingers.

She put food coloring in it.

She made a giant mess.

It was not his idea of fun.

But he still had to help his sister.

He looked around the room.

"This place is pretty clean

for a goopy crime scene," he said.

"Before we even started,

someone took the flour," Katie said.

Marty checked the door.

It was unlocked.

"We better work fast.

When did you see it last?" he asked.

"About five," Katie answered.

"When Jackie's mother called her home."

The last time Marty saw Jackie,
she was juggling garlic
and roller-skating at the same time.
"I think she's wacky,
but let's talk to Jackie," Marty said.
Marty and Katie walked next door.

The Suspects

Jackie's mother answered the door.

"Jackie's in her room," she said.

Marty and Katie went inside.

Jackie was playing her trombone.

She wore purple rain boots

and a striped ski hat.

"I'm practicing for band," Jackie explained.

"You can play all day,

but we can't stay," Marty told her.

"Why do you rhyme all the time?

It gets on my nerves," Jackie said.

Marty didn't mention
how he felt about her hat.
He asked Jackie if she had seen Katie's flour.

"Yes," Jackie answered.

"I gave it to her.

We were going to make goop."

"Pardon the poem,

but did you take it home?" Marty asked.

"Of course not," Jackie said.

"The flour was a present."

Marty whispered to Katie.

"She may be unique,

but I don't think she's a sneak."

He decided to leave before Jackie

played another song.

Marty and Katie walked past

Mr. Lynch's house.

Marty saw something on the ground.

It was a trail of white powder.

He bent down and touched it.

"It might be flour,

but it smells a bit sour," Marty said.

He and Katie followed the trail.

It led to Mr. Lynch's backyard.

Mr. Lynch was planting tulips.

Next to him was a bag that looked like flour.

Marty knelt down beside him.

He pointed to the bag.

He pointed to Katie.

"Excuse me, sir.

Did you take this from her?" Marty asked.

Mr. Lynch shook his head.

"This is a special mix," he answered.

"It helps the flowers grow."

He sprinkled some powder in the soil.

Marty remembered a poem
he had read that morning.
It was about tulips growing along
the railroad tracks.
He wanted to stay and watch Mr. Lynch,
but Katie started to walk back home.
"Mr. Lynch had flour, yes, indeed.
But just the kind that grows from seed,"
Marty said.

"You're the WORST brother,
the WORST poet,
and the WORST detective in the world,"
Katie screamed.

It was always difficult
keeping a little sister happy.

The Search Continues

Marty told Katie they should keep looking,
but first he wanted to track down a clue.
He remembered his mother was baking.
He remembered that flour went in a cake.
Maybe his mom took Katie's by mistake.
(Sometimes he even thought in rhymes.)
"Mom, we've been looking for an hour.
Have you seen Katie's flour?"
His mother opened the oven door.
She took out a beautiful yellow cake.
"I haven't seen it," his mother said.
"What was it in?"
His mother must have a lot on her mind.
Even more than Mr. Lipsky.
Marty told her the flour was in a bag.

"When you find it,

make sure you put it in some water," she said.

Marty sighed.

Even his mother wanted to make goop.

As he left the kitchen, he wondered if he

should take the cake as evidence.

He decided to wait until he solved the case.

He ran outside to find Katie.

Marty told Katie he was still looking.

"Forget it," Katie said.

"You're fired!"

"I'm not fired,

you're just feeling tired," Marty replied.

"I want a new detective!" Katie yelled.

"And a new brother!"

She ran into the house.

Marty ran to his favorite tree.

He climbed to his favorite branch.

(Climbing and rhyming

were the best things in the world.)

But now he needed to think.

He wanted to help his sister,

but his leads were running out.

Aha!

Finally Marty had a plan.

He would search the house from
the attic to the basement.

He would open every drawer, every cupboard.

He would solve this case.

From the tree, he could see Mr. Lynch's yard.

Mr. Lynch was still planting flowers.

They lined the fence in yellows and reds.

FLOWERS!

Marty had an idea.

He ran into the house.

He brought Katie into the kitchen.

He asked his mother again

if she had seen Katie's flour.

"No, I haven't," his mother answered.

"But we can pick another one tomorrow."

Marty opened the cupboard.

He took out a bag of flour.

"MY FLOUR!" Katie shouted.

"Now I can make my goop!"

Marty sang,

"Here's how I solved this tricky case—

Mom thought your flour went in a vase!"

His mother looked at the bag.

"Katie, I thought you lost a flower.

I thought you were looking

for a rose or a daisy," she said.

Now Marty understood why his mother

told him to put the flour in water.

"I needed the flour to make a cake,"

his mother said.

"I didn't know it was yours, Katie."

"Thanks, Marty," Katie said.

"Maybe you're not the worst brother after all."

Katie took the bag to the playroom.

She poured the flour into a bowl of water.

She made a gooey mess.

Katie was happy.

Marty was too.

He cut himself a huge piece of cake

and opened his poetry book.

It was his just dessert.

A Job Well Done

After dinner and homework,
Marty went to bed.
Action Chuck shared his pillow,
just in case any bad guys showed up
in his dreams.
Marty's mother came into the room.
"You solved three cases today," she said.
"Soon you won't have time for school."
"Really?" Marty jumped up in bed.
"No, not really," his mother answered.

She tucked Marty back in.

"Maybe tomorrow there will be another case,"
Marty said.

"Maybe some brand-new clues to chase,"
his mother added.

"Hey," Marty said. "You're a poet too!"

"I'm just having fun
with my detective son," she rhymed.

Then she kissed Marty
and shut off the light.

Marty went to sleep.

He dreamed that Action Chuck poured goop
along the railroad tracks.

He dreamed the bad guys
read poems until the police came.

He smiled in his sleep.

Janet Tashjian's first book, *Tru Confessions*, was hailed as a "reinvention of the diary format" in a *Publishers Weekly* starred review. She lives with her husband and young son in Needham, Massachusetts.

Laurie Keller is the author and illustrator of *The Scrambled States of America*. When she's doing her laundry, Laurie is known to spin a few rhymes of her own. She lives in New York City with her two cats.